Dear mouse friends,
Welcome to the world of

Geronimo Stilton

THE RODENT'S GAZETTE
EDITORIAL STAFF

Geronimo Stilton
A learned and brainy
mouse; editor of
The Rodent's Gazette

Thea Stilton
Geronimo's sister and
special correspondent at
The Rodent's Gazette

Trap Stilton
An awful joker;
Geronimo's cousin and
owner of the store
Cheap Junk for Less

Benjamin Stilton
A sweet and loving
nine-year-old mouse;
Geronimo's favorite
nephew

THE MISSING MOVIE

Scholastic Inc.

Published by Scholastic Inc., *Publishers since 1920*, 557 Broadway, New York, NY 10012. SCHOLASTIC and associated logos are trademarks and/or registered trademarks of Scholastic Inc.

Stilton is the name of a famous English cheese. It is a registered trademark of the Stilton Cheese Makers' Association. For more information, go to www.stiltoncheese.com.

This book is a work of fiction. Names, characters, places, and incidents are either the product of the author's imagination or are used fictitiously, and any resemblance to actual persons, living or dead, business establishments, events, or locales is entirely coincidental.

ISBN 978-1-338-54696-5

Text by Geronimo Stilton
Original title *Il mistero del film rubato*
Cover by Iacopo Bruno, Roberto Ronchi, Alessandro Muscillo, and Pietro Piscitelli
Illustrations by Danilo Barozzi, Daria Cerchi, and Serena Gianoli
Graphics by Marta Lorini

Special thanks to Anna Bloom
Translated by Anna Pizzelli
Interior design by Becky James

10 9 8 7 6 5 4 3 2 1   19 20 21 22 23

Printed in the U.S.A.   40
First printing 2019

A FESTIVAL OF SURPRISES

This morning, when the alarm clock went off, I really did not feel like getting up. My blanket was **SO WARM**, my pillow **SO soft**, my mattress **so comfy**. What a perfect day to be a *lazy mouse*! I turned the alarm off and shut my eyes again. "Just five more minutes . . ." I mumbled to myself. But before I could go back to sleep, I heard a **LOUD** noise.

Zzzzz!

RING RING RING!!!

OH NO! MY CELL PHONE! I need my beauty rest! Oh, I almost forgot to introduce myself! I am *Geronimo Stilton*, editor-in-chief of *The Rodent's Gazette*, the most famouse newspaper on Mouse Island. The news **sleeps** for no mouse, but sometimes even I need some extra **shut-eye**.

I reached over to answer the phone.

"**Good morning**," a mouselet squeaked. "I am calling from MiceOpinion, a polling company. We're asking local mice who they think will take home the top prize at this weekend's big festival."

"**FESTIVAL? WHAT FESTIVAL?**" I asked.

"You don't know about it?" she asked.

"Who's competing?" I asked.

"Sorry, time is short and I have to finish my **polling calls**. I'll put you down as undecided! Have a good day!"

She hung up. Holey Swiss cheese, what's the hurry?

But by now, I was completely awake, so I hopped out of bed, got dressed, and headed out into New Mouse City.

When I reached Mozzarella Avenue, I ran into a large crowd standing outside the GRAND HOTEL.

"I'll melt into a **PUDDLE** of cheddar if I don't get an autograph," a mouselet squeaked.

"I'm definitely getting a selfie!" another rodent called.

?! ?Who were they talking about? ?!? I wondered.

"Excuse me. What is everymouse waiting for?" I asked.

The first mouselet clutched her paws

together. "Not what — who! Noah Provoloney and Lana Ricotta, the famous **actoRS** who are staying here for the big festival!"

I had never heard of them. And there goes that **MYSTERIMOUSE FESTIVAL** again!

Before I could ask more, the crowd erupted in screams.

I was so blinded by the camera **flashes** that I could barely see the two famouse actors leaving the hotel. The crowd surged forward and my whiskers trembled. I didn't want to get **squashed** flat like a slice of American cheese!

"Help!" I squeaked.

I managed to **squeeze** out of the crowd and make my escape.

When I finally made it to my favorite breakfast spot, the barista, Flip Hotpaws,

was rushing out. He hung a SIGN on the door:

CLOSED
FOR FESTIVAL

?!? *That festival again!* **?!?**

"Sorry, Mr. Stilton. We'll see you next week!" Flip said. He shut the door so quickly, he almost snagged my snout!

SLAM!

THIS IS THE LAST CHEESE STRAW!

I got to *The Rodent's Gazette* and settled into my office. My stomach rumbled from hunger. Thankfully, I had a few **cheese sticks** from the day before stashed in a desk drawer.

You are finally here!

But right as I was about to bite into one, my assistant, **Mousella**, burst in.

"Mr. Stilton, you are finally here! Did you bring your speech for the *festival*?"

I threw down my cheese stick in frustration. "This is the last cheese straw! What in the name of all that is **furry** is this festival that everyone is squeaking about?!"

Mousella's whiskers drooped. "The **FILM FESTIVAL**, of course! It's the first one the city has ever hosted, and you agreed to give the opening speech. I left a note to remind you on your desk **THREE** days ago!"

"Me? Give a speech?" I stammered. Suddenly, my office door swung open again and my friend **CREEPELLA VON CACKLEFUR** bounded in.

"I couldn't help but overhear that you'll be delivering the opening speech! That's great news! I'm going to be

Geronimo!

Creepella!

one of the judges as the expert on **scary movies**!"

"That's fabumouse, Creepella, but I don't really think I can give this speech —"

"Of course you can! And tomorrow you can walk the **red carpet** with me!"

Right then my cousin Trap barged into my office, too. Doesn't anyone *knock* first?!

"Almost time for the big moment. **Are you ready?**"

My fur stood up on end. "How come you know about my **speech**? I don't even remember agreeing to give one! And I've never heard of this festival!"

"I know because I saw this note on your desk a few days ago. I stopped in to see you, but you weren't here." Trap pulled a wrinkled *piece of paper* from his pocket.

Dear Mr. Stilton,
Don't forget! You have to write the New Mouse City Film Festival opening speech.
Best,
Mousella

NEW MOUSE CITY FILM FESTIVAL

WHAT IS IT?

An international movie festival that runs for three days. Any rodent in New Mouse City can go see the festival movies. At the end of the festival, a panel of judges selects the best movies out of all the ones that have been screened.

WHO PLANS IT?

Jack Monterey, New Mouse City's leading film expert.

WHO DECIDES WHO THE WINNERS ARE?

The jury is composed of rodents who work in the movie industry, for example, Creepella von Cacklefur, a well-known author and scary movie director.

WHAT MOVIES ARE BEING SHOWN?

There is something for everyone!
Categories are by genre:

Whisker Tremblers
(Horror movies)

Hugs and Kisses
(Romantic movies)

Mystery Mice
(Detective movies)

Three Tissue Boxes
(Dramas)

Kaboom!
(Action movies)

WHAT ARE THE PRIZES?

There are five prizes:

Best Director
Best Actor
Best Actress
Best Screenplay
Best Overall Movie

The Golden Cheese Prize is assigned to the winner of the best-overall movie.

GOLDEN CHEESE

WHERE DOES IT TAKE PLACE?

Near the New Mouse City boardwalk, in a large building called the Movie Palace, which houses twelve movie screens.

THE MOVIE PALACE

Mousella *squeaked* in surprise. "So that's where my note went!"

My stomach dropped and I felt sweat start to build up on my whiskers. Oh dear! I was really going to have to deliver this speech after all!

Trap turned to Creepella. "Well, if Geronimo doesn't want to walk the **red carpet** with you, I'll do it. Do you know I'm shooting a documentary about the festival?"

Creepella shook her head. "I'd much rather go with Geronimo."

But Trap didn't seem to hear her. "I'm going to interview actors, directors, even festival attendees. It's going to be the most **marvemouse** documentary ever created!" He dropped to his knees. "Walk the **red carpet** with me, Creepella!"

I sighed. Trap was always so **dramatic**.
Creepella laughed. "No, thanks, Trap."
She turned to me. "I will come pick you up
tomorrow morning for the **red carpet**.
Good luck with your speech!"
SQUEAK!

You're On, Geronimo!

I went home and started writing my speech. Moldy mozzarella, it was such **HARD WORK**! I fell asleep on my laptop and woke up with a start. It was already almost time for the film festival opening!

If I *hurried*, I still had a few minutes to actually practice it before squeaking in a room full of famouse snouts.

I *SPRINTED* to the bathroom mirror and took a deep breath. "Dear ladies and gentlemice —"

I was interrupted by the doorbell.

I hurried downstairs and threw open the door. **CREEPELLA!**

She walked in holding a **fancy** dry cleaner's bag in her paws. "Are you ready yet, Geronimo? You weren't going to **wear** that, were you?" She gestured at my rumpled suit and frowned. "It looks like you **slept** in it!"

Before I could stammer out a reply, Creepella thrust the bag at me. "It's a good thing I came prepared!" She **ZIPPED** open the bag and removed a **black** suit.

"That's for me?" I asked.

"Yes, Geronimo! This speech is a big deal, and you have to look like a classy mouse! Now **shake your tail** and go get dressed!"

Resigned, I went to change. When I got back, Creepella cheered. **"You look scarily good!"**

I shook my head. "I don't know about this, Creepella. I think I look more like a **PENGUIN** than a mouse!"

Creepella rolled her eyes. "Nonsense! You look mouserific! Come on, let's go. The red carpet is waiting for us!"

I grabbed my speech and we left.

When we got to the Movie Palace, I was blown away by the size of the crowd. It looked like every **mouselet** in the city had staked out a spot along the red carpet to catch a glimpse of the actors and celebrities walking into the theater.

Slimy Swiss cheese! My stomach did flip-flops and sweat rolled down my snout. I twisted my tail in my paws. "Do you think we can go in the back way so we don't have to walk by all these **mice**?"

"Geronimo!" Creepella cried, exasperated.

"Walking by all these mice is the whole point! Come on, now. Smile for the PHOTOGRAPHERS!"

Creepella held my  and we walked down the red carpet, which was lined with photographers.

They were all shouting at us, asking us to turn left and right. Suddenly, cameras went off everywhere!

FLASH! FLASH!

I could barely see where I was going, when

BANG . . .

I hit the ground like a cheese soufflé falling off a table!

I had tripped over a LUMP in the carpet.

Oh no! I looked like such a fool!

Creepella helped me up. "Geronimo, you're such a crafty **mouse**! What a great way to make sure our pictures will be everywhere online tomorrow!"

I **GROANED**.

Creepella dragged me the rest of the way down the **red carpet** to the Movie Palace entrance. Jack Monterey, the festival's director, was waiting for us.

"Welcome and thank you for coming!"

Creepella grinned. "We're **honored** to be part of such an important event!"

We followed Jack into the theater. He showed Creepella to her seat with the rest of the jury panel and then he walked me **backstage**.

I took out my notes to practice my speech. The rodents in the audience were expecting something fabumouse!

But just then something **GRAY** and *HAIRY* swung at my head.

"Help! A **MONSTER**!" I screamed, throwing my **NOTES** up in the air.

I was about to faint from fear, when **someone familiar** peeked out from behind the monster.

"Trap!" I squeaked. "What are you doing over there? You scared the Gouda out of me!"

Trap put down his camera and boom microphone (which I had mistaken for a *HAIRY MONSTER*) and explained. "A real documentary director tries to be one with the background. That way, the subjects of the movie will act natural."

"I didn't agree to be a subject in your movie in the first place," I snapped. "And now my notes are all **mixed up**! Quick, help me put them back in the right order . . ."

But it was too late. The sound of applause erupted on the other side of the curtains. Jack Monterey's voice boomed: "And now, here is Mr. Stilton!"

"You're on, Geronimo!" Trap exclaimed, pushing me onto the stage.

WAIT, MY NOTES!

ENTER STILTON, STAGE LEFT!

I stood on the stage, my WHISKERS trembling from fear. "W-welcome to all of you." I gulped.

What in the CHEDDAR BISCUITS was I going to say without my notes?! I closed my eyes. My grandfather William always used to tell me to take a deep breath and follow my heart when I wasn't sure what to do. I remembered how he would take me to the movies when I was a mouselet. Wait! That was it! My eyes SNAPPED open.

"When I was a mouselet . . ."

The speech flowed out of me. When I was done, the audience clapped for a very long time.

Backstage, Jack patted me on the back. "Well done, Geronimo! You are a **REAL** film **enthusiast!**"

I blushed. "**Thank you!**"

Creepella bounded up and gave me an **ENORMOUSE** hug. "Geronimo, your speech made me tear up!"

"Aw, thanks," I said, **embarrassed**. Who would have guessed that Trap had done me a favor by ruining my notes?

Creepella grabbed my arm. "Now let's go! The first **SCARY** movie is about to start — *The Cheese Walks at Midnight!*"

I do not like **scary movies**. But I did not want to disappoint Creepella. So I found a way to get through it . . .

At the end of the movie, Creepella leaped up and applauded. "How **CREEPY** and marvemouse was that? Geronimo?" She

looked around but didn't see me.

"Right under here . . ." I said. I peeked my snout out from under my seat. "Is it over?" I asked.

Creepella helped me get up from under the seat. "Come on out! Another movie is about to start, RETURN OF THE ZOMBIE MOZZARELLA! You won't want to miss this one!"

OH, BUT I DID!

I grabbed the schedule and started looking for movies in the "Hugs and Kisses" category. "Hmm . . . how about we go watch *To All the Cheeses I've Loved Before,* playing in Theater 3?"

Creepella sighed. "I don't think there are any zombies in that one. But go ahead. You might pick up some **romance** tips!" She winked.

I **waved** good-bye and headed to Theater 3.

But the Movie Palace was a maze. I turned down one hallway and then another. I went up a set of stairs and then down another set of stairs. **MELTY MOZZARELLA**, I was lost!

Just when I was about to give up, I saw it: a door with a sign that read **Theater 3**.

"Finally!" I muttered, opening the door. But as I walked inside, I was blinded by a light and a **crowd** started booing. This wasn't the entrance; it was the maintenance door to the movie screen itself!

Now my ENORMOUSE shadow was blocking everyone's view.

Squeak! How embarrassing! I ran back out the way I'd come. There was another door, labeled **Projection Theater 3**, so I tried that one instead.

But it was just the room with the movie projector! The mouse

running the machine frowned and waved me out. I left so **FAST**, I almost tripped over all the wires, unplugging the whole thing!

As soon as I got out of there, I found a **THiRD** door. This one also said **Theater 3**. *Ah! This has to be the one*, I thought.

I opened the door, but instead of a darkened theater, I discovered a brightly lit dressing room! The rodent inside was getting ready to present the next **MOVIE**.

"Sorry!" I cried, and **SLAMMED** the door shut. **WAS *I* EVER GOING TO SEE THIS MOVIE?**

A LITTLE FILM HISTORY

The beginning

The first public movie screening took place in Paris on December 28, 1895, thanks to the Lumiere brothers, Louis and Auguste. It showed workers leaving a factory.

The movies looked very different then. They were all short, black and white, and silent. Many of them showed scenes from everyday life.

All aboard!

One early film showed a train pulling into a station. It's long been rumored that the audience members started to run away from the oncoming train in the movie. Although they would have been unfamiliar with moving images on-screen, there's no proof that the stampede actually occurred.

Feature films

The first feature films were created around 1910. Feature films were longer than an hour, told a story, and looked more similar to what we are used to seeing today. These first feature films were still silent and in black and white.

QUIET, PLEASE!

Films find their voice

Instead of hearing spoken dialogue, early moviegoers would read dialogue on-screen in between scenes. At the same time, a pianist or a small orchestra would play the movie soundtrack live in the theater. The first movie where audiences could actually hear the actors' voices screened in 1927 and was called *The Jazz Singer*.

Full color

Most movies produced before the 1960s were black and white. In the early 1900s, if filmmakers wanted color on-screen, they would have to have the film negatives painted by hand. Eventually, the technology advanced to film movies in color. At first, it was difficult and expensive. The cameras needed to be bigger and heavier, and the sets needed much stronger lighting. It wasn't until the 1960s that most movies were made in color!

SAY CHEESE!

I decided to take a break and relax on the boardwalk. I was in the middle of enjoying a mouse nap when a strangely dressed mouse tapped me on the shoulder.

"**Good afternoon!** I am scouting new snouts for my next movie!" he said. "Your profile is just perfect for the screen!"

I rubbed my eyes sleepily. "You want me to be in a **MOVIE?**" I looked up at the director. He seemed very familiar, but I couldn't quite place him.

Confused, I asked, "Do we know each other?"

"Nope! But what do you say; **want** to be in a movie?" He wiggled his eyebrows up and down.

I sat up. "I'm not an actor but . . ." I trailed off. In my mind, I could see GERONIMO all in lights. "Okay, what do I have to do?"

"Fabumouse!" the director cried. "The first step is to film a screen test to see what kind of acting range you have. I'll give you a series of **animals** and objects and you'll pretend to be them. **Sound good?** I'll give you five seconds to prepare."

Five seconds?! "Oh, uh, it's happening right now?"

"*ReadySetGo* — first pretend you're a **seagull** flying over the ocean!"

I flapped my arms up and down and the director grinned. "Very majestic!"

Squawk, squawk!

I PRETENDED TO BE A SEAGULL!

Vroom, vroom!

THEN A RACE CAR DRIVER,

Swish, swish!

AND THEN A PALM TREE!

"Now pretend you are a race car **driver**!"

I gripped an imaginary steering **WHEEL** and hit the gas.

"Now pretend you are a PALM TREE swaying in the *BREEZE*!"

I did as he asked, but I could see that we were starting to attract an audience.

"Isn't that Geronimo Stilton, the famouse journalist?" I heard a rodent whisper.

"You're right, that is Geronimo Stilton! What is he doing?"

One of the rodents held up her phone and took a picture.

The director wasn't finished with me. "Now pretend you are a **DINOSAUR**!"

"Enough! I don't want to be an actor anymore!" I STOMPED my feet.

To my surprise, the director burst out laughing. He reached up and pulled off his **mustache** and glasses. "Holey cheese, you should see your face, Geronimo!"

I gasped. "You're not a director, you're **Hercule Poirat**!" Hercule is the most famouse detective in New Mouse City — and my g©©d friend! What are you doing here?"

"I came to watch the **detective movies**, of course," Hercule said. "It's where I get all the **BEST** ideas for solving my most diffiₑulʈ cases!"

I crossed my 🐾🐾🐾🐾 in front of me and turned to walk back to my bench.

"Wait, Geronimo!" Hercule called. He continued: "Come see *The Mystery of the Smelly Cheese* with me."

"Well, actually, I was going to continue my nap," I replied.

"Come on, Stilton, don't be a lazy cheese ball!" he insisted, and he pulled me toward the theater.

At the end of the MOVIE, my whiskers were trembling. This movie was even SCARIER than the scary movie had been!

Hercule didn't seem scared at all, however. "That director is a real genius!"

"I liked her FIRST movie, *The Malted Milk Falcon*, better," said a voice behind us.

Hercule and I turned around and saw a mouselet in a blue dress.

"Frozen feta!" Hercule cried. "I love *The Malted Milk Falcon*!"

Hercule and the mouselet launched into a long conversation about the movies directed by Angelica Whiskerton. She was a supermouse film director. But I was **exhausted**.

I was about to FALL ASLEEP, when the mouselet turned to me. "What kind of movies do you like?" she asked.

"Well —" I started.

"There you are, Geronimo!" Creepella called. She RUSHED up to us. "I've been looking all over for you! I waited **forever** outside Theater 3!"

"Oh, sorry!" I said. *"To All the Cheeses I've Loved Before* was full, so I waited out here."

"Let's go, Geronimo! Tomorrow, we just won't split up." Creepella gestured for me to follow her.

"T-t-tomorrow?" I stammered.

"Of course!" Creepella exclaimed: "The festival lasts three days!"

SQUEAK! How was I going to sit through three days of scary movies?!

Where have you been?

Sorry!

Movie Mix-Up!

The following morning, Creepella greeted me on my doorstep. "Are you excited for the world premiere of scary-movie director Mousen Scorsese's SUPER-SECRET MOVIE!"

What? I didn't have a clue what she was talking about!

"Is it going to be very scary?" I asked.

"Yes!" Creepella cried. "His **scariest** one yet! I can't wait. And we get to watch it sitting right next to each other!"

When we got to the theater where the *TOP SECRET* movie would be shown, the seats were almost filled. We grabbed the last two empty spots and got **comfortable**. All around us, rodents were excitedly chatting about the MOVIE.

"I hope this is as good as the last one!" the mouse next to us said.

Then the lights dimmed, and all the chatting stopped. I gripped the sides of my seat. I hoped it wouldn't scare my fur off!

The movie's first scene flickered onto the SCREEN.

A cartoon CAT family sat around a table. This didn't look scary at all!

A sudden cry rang out: "This is not my film!"

All the lights went up, and a rodent with long WHITE FUR ran toward the projection room.

"That was the director," Creepella exclaimed. "Let's go see what happened."

Inside the projector room, the director was yelling and waving his 🐾🐾🐾🐾.

"Is this some kind of a joke? What did you

do with my movie?!"

The projectionist scurried around, checking all the equipment. "It looks like someone deleted the file of your movie and downloaded this one," the projectionist said. "It wasn't me. I was working in another theater."

Jack nodded. "I believe you. I was with him," he told the director. "Let's just find a way to fix this before we track down the **rascally rat** who did it."

THE PROJECTIONIST

The projectionist is the person who operates the movie projector. He or she prepares the equipment, makes sure that the images and sound are clear, and checks that the projection of the motion picture fits correctly on the movie screen.

"I'll need the **backup drive** where the original file was saved," the projectionist said.

"It's in the safe right over here," Jack said.
"WHAT ARE WE WAITING FOR?!" Mousen yelled.

"Open that safe!"

Jack punched his code in. But then he gasped. "**The backup drive is not here!**" he shouted.

"What?" Mousen turned as WHITE as a bowl of cheese soup. "That was the only copy!"

I SMELL A MYSTERY!

Suddenly, a familiar snout strode into the room.

"I smell a mystery!" Hercule cried, rubbing his 🐾🐾🐾🐾 together. "What is going on?"

"Hercule, how did you know something had gone wrong at the festival?" I asked.

"Whenever there is a mystery to be solved, my whiskers tickle!"

Hercule began to inspect the room using a **magnifying glass**. "No sign of a break-in . . . no 🐾🐾🐾🐾🐾🐾🐾🐾🐾 **ANYWHERE** . . . strange . . . do you agree, Stilton?"

Before I could respond, my cousin Trap suddenly appeared, carrying his **video camera** on his shoulder.

"I came as soon as I heard!" he cried, huffing and puffing from rushing. "This is **MOUSERIFIC**!"

I frowned, my whiskers twitching. "This is nothing to be **happy** about!"

"Someone has *stolen* the most anticipated movie of the year . . . and I am the only one who has been filming all along! I can help crack the case — and film a *fabumouse* documentary in the process!"

Creepella stalked over. "Enough chitchat," she hissed. "We have to find out what happened!"

My eyes widened: "We? Who's 'we'?" I asked.

"You and me, of course!" Creepella cried.

"We could all work together!" Hercule said: "Come on, Geronimo! It will be *fun*! And I'm the **BEST** detective in town, so you'll all be in very good 🐾🐾🐾🐾."

I was outnumbered! But suddenly, I realized that if I was solving an actual mystery, I would not have to sit through any more terrifying film mysteries! "Fine!" I said. "Where do we start?"

"Why don't I go check with the security team here and see if the cameras in this room caught anything suspicious?" Creepella suggested.

"What a smart idea!" Hercule rejoiced.

"I will walk on the boardwalk to film interviews with festival-going mice!" Trap said. "Some rodents might have seen something odd."

"What a great idea!" Hercule cheered.

I didn't want to be left out. "We should question the director to find out more information about his TOP SECRET MOVIE!" I suggested.

"I have an idea!" Hercule said. "We should question the director to find out more information about his **TOP SECRET MOVIE**!"

I shook my snout. "That was **MY IDEA!**" But Hercule just headed out of the room.

"Let's go, Geronimo! We have a mystery to solve!"

We all followed Hercule out of the projection room and split up. Trap turned to go outside to the boardwalk and Creepella went to check the Movie Palace security cameras.

Tea is very calming!

Hercule and I found the famouse director drinking cheddar leaf tea at the Movie Palace cafe.

"I find a nice cup

of hot cheddar tea very **calming**," he told us as we sat down.

Hercule leaned across the table. "Was that really the only copy of your movie that the thief took?"

Director Mousen Scorsese sighed heavily. "It was! I did not want any rodents getting their 🐾🐾🐾🐾 on it! And I hoped that by advertising the fact that there was only one copy, it would make it seem **extra top secret**!"

The director seemed even more **glum** when he saw the look on my face. "There's

Mousen Scorsese

PROFESSION: Director
MOST FAMOUSE MOVIE:
Goudafellas
AWARDS: The Silver Camera,
The Golden Grater

no use talking about this anymore. The film is gone, and it could be **DANGEROUS** to go after the thief."

My whiskers trembled. "Dangerous?! Why?!"

But **MOUSEN** just shook his head. "I can't say more than that," he said, looking down at his tea.

We said our good-byes and met **CREEPELLA** in the security camera control room.

"I discovered that the security cameras were disabled at 8:00 p.m. yesterday," she explained.

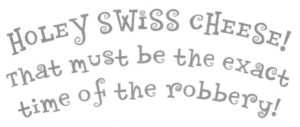

HOLEY SWISS CHEESE! That must be the exact time of the robbery!

INTERVIEW WITH A RODENT

I thought about the strange conversation we had with Mousen. Who didn't want the movie to be screened? And why would he not want us to go after the thief? He had said it could be **DANGEROUS**. I didn't want to get hurt!

Hercule paced UP AND DOWN the control room. "Someone must be mad at Mousen," he said. "If we can find out which rodents have been arguing with him recently, I bet we can unmask the thief!"

"I'm afraid you'll have to keep working without me," Creepella said, checking the time. "Jury duty is calling me. I have to see another **MOVIE**." I walked her to the door.

"See you later!" She waved at the two of us and *DASHED* off.

When I went back, Hercule was studying his tablet. I peered over his shoulder and saw that he was doing an internet search on Mousen Scorsese.

I sat down in a nearby chair and waited for him to finish. I had almost drifted off to **sleep** when Hercule yelped. "Clattering cat tails!"

I fell out of my chair. **SPLAT!**

Hercule chuckled. "Geronimo, you are such a **clumsy cheese wheel**! Do you want to know what I just discovered?"

I rubbed my snout. "**Of course!**"

He turned his tablet toward me so that I could see the screen. "**Check this out.**"

I squinted at the screen. The article headline was "Mousen Scorsese and His Enemies." Rancid ricotta! This was just what we needed.

Hercule scrolled down. "The article names THREE rodents he's had arguments with."

"WOW!" I squeaked.

"It gets better," Hercule said. He switched over to a festival guest list the organizers had emailed him. "His THREE WORST enemies are all here at the festival this weekend!"

FESTIVAL GUESTS

1. Toasty Fontina
2. Ronaldo Crostini
3. Albus Mackintosh

"We have to find them and talk to them!" I said. "But how will we do that?"

"Easy," Hercule said, peeling a banana. "I already know where they are! They are all staying at the GRAND HOTEL."

"How do you know that?" I asked.

Hercule winked. "Am I not the BEST detective in town? Now let's go to the hotel!"

I rolled my eyes and followed Hercule as he made his way out of the *Movie Palace*. We were just about to leave through the front doors when we spotted the mouselet Hercule had been chatting with earlier.

"What a coincidence!" he squeaked, waving his paw.

They immediately started talking about detective movies again. I felt my mind drifting. Maybe no one would notice if I snuck off for a quick mouse nap . . .

"What about you, GERONIMO?" the mouselet asked me, snapping me back into the conversation. "Which MOVIES have you seen so far?"

"UM . . . WELL . . ." I did not want to lie, but I didn't want to tell a **STRANGE** mouselet that I hadn't seen many because I was investigating the **MISSING MOVIE CASE**, either.

But Hercule didn't seem to mind sharing. "Actually, we have been working on the **MISSING MOVIE CASE**! I am sure you **HEARD** about Mousen Scorsese's stolen film!"

Just then Creepella came up next to us. "What are you doing just standing around? This **mystery** isn't going to solve itself! The festival will be ruined if we can't get the **MOVIE** back.

Hello!

Oh no!

"I'm on the jury, GERONIMO. This festival is important to me. If this mystery isn't solved, we won't get to do another one next year."

"You're totally right, Creepella," I said. "We'll work **faster**, I promise!"

Hercule rubbed his snout thoughtfully. "You can't *RUSH* good detecting," he said.

CREEPELLA stalked off to the next **MOVIE**. Hercule suddenly noticed that the movie-loving **mouseLet** we had been

Oh no!

talking to had disappeared.

"Oh no," Hercule wailed. "I still haven't gotten her name!"

"Come on, Hercule, let's go!" I said. "I'll buy you a nice BANANA on the way."

Hercule sighed. "Okay. But I want one dipped in **chocolate** this time. And sprinkles! Wait, make that **two** bananas!"

Squeak!

THE ENEMIES LIST!

When we got to the Grand Hotel, I strolled up to the reception desk. "Good morning. I am Geronimo. It's a pleasure to meet you. We would like to **TALK** to director Toasty Fontina, please," I said.

He smiled and picked up the desk telephone and called up to **TOaSty FONtiNa'S** room.

"He'll meet you in the lobby in **Five** minutes," the receptionist said, hanging up the phone.

Five minutes later, a VERY SHARPLY DRESSED rodent walked toward us. We **introduced** ourselves and then we sat on the sofa by the front door.

"What can I do for you?" Fontina asked.

"I'll cut to the cheese," Hercule said. "We're looking for Mousen Scorsese's stolen film. We've heard you and the director aren't very **friendly** with each other."

Fontina grunted. "That's putting it **mildly**. We used to be friends, but now we don't even **TALK**!" His **WHISKERS** shook with the intensity of his anger. "I certainly didn't **STEAL** his movie, but I can't say I'm sorry to see him have a **hard** time at the **festival**."

Let me handle this, Stilton!

Ouch!

He seemed sincere. But how could we believe him when he said he didn't steal the movie? "Why are you **so upset** with him?" I asked.

"Look," Fontina said.

TOASTY FONTINA

PROFESSION: Film director
MOST FAMOUS MOVIE: *Treasure of the Lost Rodents*
AWARDS: The Golden Reel, The Big Cheese

"Mousen's movies are good, but they are not as *fabumouse* as my movies. It's about time I took home the **big prize**!"

I coughed and looked down so that Fontina couldn't see me **ROLL MY EYES**. All these directors had such big **cheddarheads**!

"Where were you last night around **8:00 P.M.**?" Hercule asked.

The director shrugged. "Where anyone who is anyone in this town was."

"At the **party** for the ninetieth birthday

of the great director Otto Mouseburg, of course! It started around 8:00 p.m. last night." He took out his cell phone and opened his photos. "Look!"

HE WAS TELLING THE TRUTH!

HE COULD NOT BE THE THIEF!

HOLEY SWISS CHEESE!

After Fontina left, Hercule and I compared notes. We agreed that the photos proved his alibi. We'd have to move on to the second rodent on our suspect list.

"Ronaldo Crostini!" Hercule cried. There he was now, strolling across the hotel lobby. "What a coincidence!"

He *DASHED* over to the actor and led the young rodent back to our sofa.

We explained who we were and what we were looking for. Crostini's snout wrinkled into a frown. "You know what? I am happy his movie was stolen!"

Holey Swiss cheese! There was no love lost between these two rodents!

"Why are you so angry with him?" Hercule asked.

"IT'S NO SECRET THAT WE HAD A FALLING OUT. He promised me the lead role in his film *Race to Cheese Mountain*. I missed a few rehearsals and I forgot to call and let him know. When I came in for the first day of shooting, I learned that he'd given my part to another actoR!"

"That must have made you MAD," I said. "MAD enough to want to sabotage his big premiere, even."

Ronaldo Crostini

PROFESSION: Actor
MOST FAMOUSE MOVIE: *Hairy Mouser and the Cheesemonger's Secret*
AWARDS: The Golden Paw, the Palm de Brie

Crostini smiled the smile that had made him *famouse* around the world. "Mousen and I may be **ENEMIES**, but I'm no **thief**. Last night when the robbery occurred I was visiting my **granny mouse**. She makes the best **cheese pie** in all of New Mouse City!"

Hercule **MELTED** like a cheese stick in the sun. "Mmm, cheese pie! Maybe we should all go see her right now!"

Crostini looked down at his phone. "Oh, it looks like she's calling me now. Will you excuse me? I have to let her know I will not be able to go see her tonight."

After we said **good-bye**, Hercule and I walked back to the reception desk.

Hercule twirled his WHISKERS thoughtfully. "It will be easy to check his alibi.

I think he's telling the truth, though. That means there's only **one** more suspect left on our list!"

FILM EDITOR

The editor puts together shots of different scenes in the order that the director wants them.

I looked down at the list. Albus Mackintosh, a film editor, was the last rodent we had to question. We had the receptionist call up to his room for us and headed back to our interviewing sofa.

Mackintosh showed up a few minutes later and Hercule wasted no time in launching into why we had asked him **down** here.

"My name is **Hercule Poirat** and I am the most *famouse* detective in New Mouse City. I am **INVESTIGATING** Mousen Scorsese's missing movie!"

Mackintosh sighed. "I don't want to hear

anything about that ridiculous director! He hired me to **EDIT** his movie *Gone with the Cheese Grater* over and over again.

Albus Mackintosh

PROFESSION:
Film editor
FAMOUSE MOVIE:
Where the Cheesy Things Are
AWARDS:
The Perfect Slice for Best Chase Sequence

"It took **forever**! And then, after everything was almost done, he **FIRED** me and took my name off the credits!" Mackintosh's ears drooped.

"Why would he **FIRE** you, if you were almost finished with the film?" I asked.

"I made a couple of **mistakes** in the editing process," Mackintosh explained. "I could have fixed it, if he'd let me! But he's a **perfectionist**. I don't know how he finds rodents who still agree to work with him. Serves him right to have his movie stolen!"

Hercule leaned in. "Where were you last night at 8:00?"

"At 8:00? Let's see, I went for a **RUN** on the boardwalk, and stopped to **chat** with a strange mouse who was filming a documentary about the **festival**. Trent, I think his name was? Or Tappy? Oh, Trap!"

I put my snout in my paws.

His alibi was my cousin Trap!

"Find him and ask him if you don't believe me!"

"Oh, I know where to **FIND** him," I said. We thanked Mackintosh for his time and left the hotel.

Now what?!

KNOCK IT OFF, CHEESEBRAIN!

Hercule left me at a *cafe* on the boardwalk. I ordered an iced cheddar chai and started thinking about the facts of the case:

1 The movie had been removed from the projector and was stolen from the safe after 8:00 p.m. on the first day of the festival.

2 Mousen Scorsese did not want to even talk about his movie.

3 The three main suspects all had strong alibis for the time of the theft.

A waiter interrupted my thoughts. "Here is your iced cheddar chai!" I turned around and recognized Hercule, disguised as a waiter. "What are you doing?" I hissed.

"I'm undercover, of course!" Hercule whispered. "In my favorite detective movie, the hero dresses like a waiter to eavesdrop on all the suspects."

Hercule launched into a very detailed description of the plot, but I zoned out. I really don't like **detective movies**!

Finally Hercule finished talking. "You

Here is your iced cheddar chai!

What are you doing?

should watch the **MOVIE**! It's actually showing at the festival this weekend, as part of the *Old Favorites* lineup in Theater 6!"

"You know I don't like detective movies. And you already told me how it ends!"

Just then Trap showed up at the cafe carrying his camera equipment. "Here you are! Have you found out anything new?"

I shook my head so hard my whiskers vibrated. "Nothing! **The three main suspects all have ironclad alibis!** And we're out of leads."

"Don't give up so fast, cheddarbrain!" Hercule cried. "I have a fabumouse idea! I will go undercover as a **ticket seller** and poke around for some new information. That's what happened in the movie *The Brie Connection,* which I watched yesterday."

Before Hercule could tell us the plot of the whole movie, I asked Trap to update us on his **documentary**.

"It's going well, Geronimo! Do you want to see a **FEW** clips?"

We nodded and Trap jumped up to get his laptop.

"You are going to love it!" he squeaked. He was so excited to show us his work.

Here it is!

FR◉STED FETA!
...It w◎s s◎ c◎nfusing!

Most of the images were **blurry**, some of the shots were upside down, the audio was **fuzzy** ... **What were we even looking at??**

Hercule seemed riveted, however. While he looked through the clips, I thought I'd try to give Trap a little gentle film **feedback**. "Trap, maybe you should reshoot some of these scenes. It's a little difficult to figure out what's going on, don't you think?"

Trap **shrugged**. "You just don't get it, Geronimo! This is the way **REAL LIFE** is — fast, **blurry**, hard to hear! My documentary has to stay true to the festival. The blurry shots and **fuzzy** audio show just how energetic the film festival is — it can barely be contained on video!"

Clearly Trap was not interested in my opinion! I looked over Hercule's shoulder. "Creepella is in focus in some of these, at least," I said.

"But of course!" he exclaimed. "She's the **STAR** of my documentary. I used a special effect to make sure the main character would stand out!"

"Quiet, both of you **cheesebrains**!" Hercule shouted. He stood up dramatically.

"I KNOW WHO STOLE THE MOVIE!"

To Catch a Mouse!

We stared at Hercule in **shock**. He gestured for us to gather around the laptop.

"Look at this." He clicked on **PLAY** and a video started. It had a time stamp of **8:00 P.M.** the night before. I could tell right away that we were looking at the door to the projection room where Scorsese's **MOVIE** had been stolen!

It was a little hard to see, but three things were clear:

1 A mouselet walked to the **security camera** and moved it.

2 Then took the keys from the projectionist, who didn't notice.

3 Next, she walked into the room and **walked out** shortly after.

4 Lastly, she dropped the keys near the PROJECTIONIST'S feet.

I could not believe my eyes . . .

"Can you **ZOOM** in on her?" I asked. Trap took over at the laptop keyboard and changed some of the settings.

"Here you go," he said, hitting **PLAY** again.

I gasped.

"Do you know her?" Trap asked.

The mouselet on-screen was the detective movie fan Hercule and I had talked to!

"We've **met** her," I explained to Trap. "But we never caught her name. I can't believe you filmed the **whole** crime! I thought you were out on the **BOARDWALK** all last night filming interviews!"

AUD SUB

THE ROBBERY

1 The mouselet tampers with the security camera.

2 She takes the keys from the projectionist.

3 She sneaks into the control room.

4 Then, after a few minutes, quiet as a mouse, walks out.

5 She gets close to the projectionist and drops his keys right next to him.

6 Finally, the projectionist picks up the keys from the floor.

Trap blushed. "I was supposed to be, but I had forgotten my camera outside the changing room. When I came back to get it, I discovered I had left it running."

Hercule shook his head sadly. "She seemed so nice! I've never met anyone who liked detective movies as much as I do!"

"We have to track down this mystery mouselet," I said.

Trap shook his head. "She's probably already far away by now. She has the secret movie — why would she stick around the **scene of the crime**?"

I wasn't so sure about that. "We saw her today. She could have left right away and disappeared with the movie. But for some reason, she hasn't."

"She probably wants to see the rest of the detective movies playing at the festival!

They're showing some films you can't see anywhere else!"

I **ROLLED** my eyes.

"No, really," Hercule insisted. "This morning she told me she was planning to see the **LATEST MOVIE** by the great director Frances Romano, *The Spy Who Loved Cheese.*"

"What are we waiting for?" I cried. I picked up the festival schedule and frantically flipped through the pages. **Why did they have to be showing so many movies?!**

"There it is!" Hercule said, pointing. "*The Spy Who Loved Cheese*! 4:45 p.m., Theater 2!"

"Let's get this cheese wheel **rolling**!" I said. "The movie is about to end!"

THE SPY WHO
LOVED CHEESE

4:45 P.M., THEATER 2

MYSTERY MOUSELET UNMASKED!

We ran all the way to Theater 2 and arrived as the audience was **EXITING** the movie. At first, I was *worried* we had missed the mysterious mouselet, but suddenly Trap *squeaked*, "There she is! You go and confront her. I will film everything for my documentary!" he said.

Hercule shook his snout. "Let's not *RUSH* into this. Look, she's calling someone! Thanks to the fabumouse Super Ear *Listening Device* invented by a friend of mine, we can hear *EVERYTHING* she says!"

Hercule turned the device on and the mouselet's voice crackled through its speaker. We could hear **every word**!

"Yes, everything went according to plan . . . No, Stilton and that cheesebrain friend of his have no idea. See you in five minutes."

The mouselet got off the phone and looked around. Suddenly, she started walking toward the boardwalk.

We quietly *followed* her all the way to a cafe, where she sat down at a table.

My WHiSKeRS were shaking from fear. Who was she going to meet?

We crept closer and hid behind a bush. A few minutes passed and a very **long**, **leopard-print** car with dark tinted windows arrived. A familiar mouselet got out, followed by two large mouseguards. I gasped.

Madame No!

"**Moldy mozzarella sticks!**" I squeaked. Madame No was a famous business rodent. She was involved in many shady dealings all over Mouse Island. We had butted snouts **many** times before!

Madame No greeted the thief, who put her **BAG** on the table opposite Madame No.

"That must be the movie!" Hercule exclaimed. "Quick! **Distract them** and I will get the bag!" Before I could stammer out a reply, Hercule was GONE.

"How are we going to distract them?" I whispered to Trap.

"Don't worry," Trap said confidently. "This will be cheeSy bReezy." He started walking toward the table, his camera on his shoulder and a microphone in his paw!

"Wait for me!" I hissed, and scampered after him. I couldn't let him walk into the paws of danger alone!

Trap approached Madame No. "Good evening, my dear mouselets!"

Madame No frowned at Trap. When she noticed me next to him, her expression deepened into a SCOWl. "Stilton!" she growled. "We meet again!"

"We, uh, do. Um, marvemouse to see you again," I lied. "Madame No, we are shooting a documentary about the local film festival and would like to ask you a few questions!"

Madame No waved her 🐾🐾🐾 in the air. "I don't have time for this — Rocky! Blue!" Two of Madame No's mouseguards came out from the SHADOWS. "Help these rodents back out to the boardwalk."

Both mouseguards walked toward us. Where was Hercule?! I tried to stall a little longer. "It'll only take a minute! The documentary will be much more interesting with a quote from a business EXPERT like yourself!"

Madame No crossed her paws in front of her. "Stilton, you are such a pest!" she hissed.

But the mysterimouse mouselet held up her paw to stop the mouseguards' approach.

"Wait! I'm a **film lover**, as you know. You could ask me your questions!"

My hunch had been right: A **REAL FILM EXPERT** would not want to miss out on an opportunity to talk about movies!

Trap adjusted his camera and I **struggled** to think of a question.

"Um, well, why don't you tell me what has been your *favorite* movie of the festival."

The thief was about to reply, when I saw a flash of **YELLOW** fly by.

IT WAS . . . A WALKING BUSH?!

Trap saw the look on my snout and nudged me with his elbow.

It was Hercule, undercover!

Hercule the bush was very close to the bag. Slowly,

he *reached out* with his paw from inside the bush and . . .

One of Madame No's **mouseguards** lunged in front of the bush and the other one searched through it. Then he pulled Hercule up by one of his ears! "**GOTCHA!**"

"**OUCH! OUCH!**" Hercule squeaked. **We were caught!**

TOASTED TUNA MELT!

The mysterimouse mouselet was shocked. "I know you. You're the rodent who's a big fan of **detective** movies."

"That's me!" Hercule replied, still dangling from the mouseguard's giant paw. "By the way, how was that Frances Romano movie?"

"QUIET, EVERYONE!" Madame No shrieked. "What's going on here? Why are you hiding in that bush?"

Trap got right to the point. "The two of you took Mousen Scorsese's movie!" he cried.

Madame No burst out laughing. "What in the name of all that is **mousey** makes you say that? You have no **proof**!"

"Madame No is right!" the mystermiouse

mouselet agreed. "Now, if you don't mind, we were just about to enjoy some fresh cheddar scones —"

"I have everything on camera," Trap cried, interrupting her. He played the recording on the camera screen for all of us.

The mysterimouse mouselet stood up from her seat. "Looks like the game is up, Madame No." In a FLASH, she had removed her wig, sunglasses, and blue dress, revealing a sleek black suit underneath.

Toasted tuna melt! It was Shadow, the most famous thief on Mouse Island!

"Yes, I did steal the **backup drive** Mousen Scorsese's movie was saved on!"

"But **WHY**?" I asked.

But before Shadow could answer, I heard a frustrated squeak from behind me.

"There you are, Geronimo. It took me

forever to find you! You haven't been answering my calls," Creepella said.

"I'm sorry," I said. "My battery died!"

"A likely story," Creepella huffed. "I think you're actually happy that Mousen Scorsese's movie got stolen, because now you have an excuse not to participate in the *festival* with me!" She angrily adjusted her purse and accidently **BONKED** me right in the snout! **OUCH!**

I turned to rub my snout and tripped over one of the cafe's chairs. The chair fell into the mouseguard holding Hercule's ear and his **sunglasses** clattered to the ground.

"On no, my **sunglasses**!" he yelled. He released Hercule's ear and leaned down to pick them up. "These are limited edition Chet Cheesington's," he **GROWLED**. He gently brushed **sand** from the lenses.

Despite the confusion, I noticed SHADOW trying to sneak the camera away from my cousin.

"Trap! Your camera!" I called.

Trap held on tight to his camera as Shadow attempted to yank it out of his paws.

"LET GO!" Trap yelled.

"Never!" Shadow cried in response. "You can kiss your evidence good-bye!" With that, she suddenly stopped pulling on the camera. Trap reeled backward in surprise and the camera fell out of his paws.

The camera smashed into a THOUSAND PIECES.

Shadow burst out laughing. "Good-bye to your little movie!" She tossed a

Never!

Let go!

smoke bomb onto the ground, and the air around us quickly filled with **CLOUDS** of thick **GRAY** smoke.

I couldn't see anything! Where was everyone?

By the time the smoke cleared, Shadow **had vanished**!

"My camera," Trap said sadly, looking at the pieces smashed on the ground. But then

My camera!

his face hardened and he pointed a paw past me. "Look! **Madame No is getting away, too!**"

Madame No had grabbed the bag containing the **backup drive** and started running to her car together with her mouseguards.

Rancid rat tails, the thieves were *GETTING AWAY* right from under our snouts!

Good-bye!

THE BACKUP IS BACK!

Madame No's car screeched away from the curb. As the **smoke** bomb cleared around us, I could finally see everyone's disappointed expressions.

"I'm sorry about your snout, Geronimo," Creepella said. "Is it feeling okay?"

"I'm fine," I said. My snout might be feeling better, but I was *sad* that Shadow had gotten the best of us again. I sighed.

"My camera!" Trap wailed. "Mousefully I had plugged in a **backup drive**, so I have a copy of everything I've recorded so far. Otherwise everything would be **LOST**!"

Trap started looking for the backup drive among the pieces of the broken camera.

Hercule coughed. "Um, Trap, I have to tell you something, but you have to promise you will not get MAD?"

"YES, I promise!" Trap said.

"Do you also promise that we will always be friends no matter what?"

"SURE, okay."

Hercule grinned. "There's good news and bad news. First the good news: In all the chaos of the smoke bomb, I was able to retrieve Mousen Scorsese's backup drive with the stolen film from Madame No's bag."

He reached into his raincoat and pulled it out.

"You are a GENIUS," Trap cried, patting him on the back. "But what is the bad news?"

"Well . . . in order to make sure Madame No didn't notice, I had to substitute this

Mouserific!

My movie!

We solved the case!

drive with another one . . . so I used yours."

Trap turned as WHITE AS A SLICE OF MOZZARELLA CHEESE. "My movie! That was the only copy! I lost my documentary forever! I will never win the Golden Cheese!"

"But we solved the case!" Creepella said. "Just think about the expression on Madame No's snout when she realizes she doesn't have the MOVIE!"

"I wonder why she didn't want anyone to see the film?" I asked.

"Maybe the reason will be clearer once we see the

movie," Creepella suggested. "Now it can be the closing movie of the festival!"

The following day the main theater was packed with rodents eager to see the secret movie — finally!

MOUSEN SCORSESE had been completely shocked when we returned his missing backup drive. "I never thought I'd get this back," he said. "Thank you again from the bottom of my **heart**!"

"You're welcome!" I said. "I can't wait to see it."

The director winked. "Now you will see why Madame No went to so much trouble to get her 🐾🐾🐾🐾 on it."

My whiskers trembled. I hoped it would not be too **scary** for me. SQUEAK!

JUST SAY NO TO MADAME NO:
A Pollution Story
by Mousen Scorcese

① EGO industries factories dump waste in a river.

② Their bulldozers clear out a forest in a protected park.

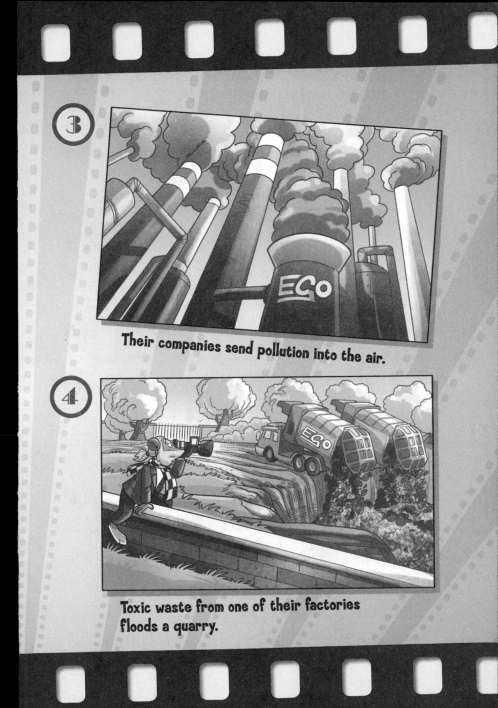

③ Their companies send pollution into the air.

④ Toxic waste from one of their factories floods a quarry.

AND THE GOLDEN CHEESE GOES TO . . .

Mousen Scorsese's secret film was not a HORROR film at all, but a documentary! He finally had proof that Madame No's factories were illegally polluting Mouse Island. It had been whispered about for years, but no one had hard evidence before now. That's why Madame No had wanted to steal it.

When the credits rolled, the audience enthusiastically clapped.

Shadow, a talented spy and thief, must have heard through her criminal networks what the SECRET film was really about, and told Madame No. They often worked together on criminal schemes.

"I can't wait to discuss this film with

all the other members of the jury!" Creepella said.

She followed the other jury mice out of the theater. It was time for them to pick the winner of the **FILM** festival!

They only deliberated for a few minutes. Sooner than everyone was expecting, they were called back into the theater.

Jack Monterey walked onto the stage and addressed the crowd. "Ladies and gentlemice, thank you for being a part of New Mouse City's very **FiRST** film festival!"

"I am very **proud** to announce that the winner of the *Golden Cheese* for best overall film is . . . Mousen Scorsese's *Just Say No to Madame No!*"

Scorsese leaped to his paws and rushed onto the stage. He wiped away a **TEAR**. "I'm honored to accept this award. I would like to *share* this award with Trap Stilton, Hercule Poirat, and Geronimo Stilton! They worked hard to help me show this movie at this festival. I'm going to strive to be more like them in the future."

What?! I looked up to see Mousen gesturing for **US** to join him on stage.

Trap wasted no time in **bounding** up to the stage and throwing his arms around Mousen. Creepella grabbed my 🐾🐾🐾 and pulled me on-stage. "Come on, Geronimo!" she cried.

Hercule joined us on-stage. "If only your sister, Thea, could see me now!"

Jack handed the Golden Cheese to me. "Why don't you do the honors of handing over the trophy?" he suggested.

I turned toward Scorsese, my whiskers trembling from happiness. "I am **happy**

to present you with this Golden Cheese —"
I began.

SUDDENLY, photographers' camera flashes
were **ALL** going off at the same time and
blinding me . . .

My vision got **blurry**. I shook my snout
to try and clear it, but that just made me
dizzy! I could tell the prize was slipping
from my paws . . . but I couldn't seem to
stop it!

"Geronimo!" Creepella cried. She grabbed
the **prize** as it
started to fall and
handed it back
to me. "Got
it, Geronimo!
What would you
do without me?"
She winked.

"Thanks!" I **whispered**, before handing it off to Mousen.

When we got off the stage, a **LARGE** crowd of fans formed around the director. Mousefully, no one was paying attention to me! I was **glad** to have helped find Scorsese's **STOLEN** movie, but I'd seen enough here to know that I'm not cut out for the **MOVIE** business!

The Rodent's Gazette
The most famous newspaper on Mouse Island
JUST SAY "NO" TO POLLUTION!
EGO Industries to Pay Massive Fine

I couldn't wait to head back to *The Rodent's Gazette* office and get started on an article about *Madame No*. She may have gotten away this time, but she couldn't run forever!

Yours truly,
Geronimo Stilton

HOW TO CREATE A MOVIE

DEAR FRIENDS,

Making a movie is a very interesting process! Here is what I learned about the movie business at the New Mouse City Film Festival!

THE PRODUCER

The producer oversees a movie project. He or she helps figure out how the movie will be financed.

2 THE SCREENPLAY

A screenplay is like a book. It has all the dialogue the actors will speak on-screen. It also describes the setting for each scene.

Just Say No to Madame No

SCREENPLAY

③ THE CAST AND CREW

Once the screenplay is finished, the cast and crew members who are involved in actually making the movie are hired.

The cast is the group of actors who will be in the movie. In addition to the main actors, there are also extras, people who are in the background of some scenes but don't speak any lines of dialogue.

The crew is all the people behind the scenes who help make the movie. This can include the director, camera operators, sound technicians, makeup artists, costume designers, production designers, and assistants.

④ THE SET AND SHOOTING THE FILM

The set is the place where the scenes are filmed. It could be a studio, a theater, or a public place like a park. People film movies in all kinds of places!

When everything is ready . . . Lights! Camera! Action!

FUN FACT!
The director begins the filming of each scene with these words: "Quiet on the set! Lights! Camera! Action!"

The director is in charge of the filming. His or her unique personal style transforms the screenplay from written words to moving images.

For every finished movie scene you see on-screen, the director might have tried many multiple different styles. For example, a wide shot to see the whole set, a medium shot to see the characters in their surroundings, or a close-up to see the actors' facial expressions clearly.

In addition to changing the kind of camera shot, the director can also ask actors to repeat their lines in different ways. Angry! Sad! Happy!

WIDE SHOT
Sets the scene.

MEDIUM SHOT
You can clearly see the actors, but the location is still important.

CLOSE-UP
Only the actors' snouts are visible in the frame, so that their feelings are the main focus.

 EDITING

After the filming is finished, what happens to the hours and hours of footage that the director has shot? All the material is handed over to the editor. The editor, together with the director, picks the best shots and assembles them in the order written in the screenplay. Editing can be a very creative part of the movie process: Sometimes entire scenes are cut, or the movie is made longer or shorter.

POSTPRODUCTION

These are tasks that are undertaken after the movie has been edited and include music and sound effects, visual effects, and voice-over narration.

7 DISTRIBUTION

Once postproduction is over, the movie is ready to be shown to movie fans. A distribution agency sends copies of the movie to the theaters that will screen it. The distribution agency takes care of the promotion as well, including submitting the movie to film festivals and organizing and planning actors' interviews. Anything to make the movie a success!

Now sit back and enjoy the show!

Don't miss a single fabumouse adventure!

Up Next:

Don't miss any of my adventures in the Kingdom of Fantasy!

THE KINGDOM OF FANTASY

THE QUEST FOR PARADISE:
THE RETURN TO THE KINGDOM OF FANTASY

THE AMAZING VOYAGE:
THE THIRD ADVENTURE IN THE KINGDOM OF FANTASY

THE DRAGON PROPHECY:
THE FOURTH ADVENTURE IN THE KINGDOM OF FANTASY

THE VOLCANO OF FIRE:
THE FIFTH ADVENTURE IN THE KINGDOM OF FANTASY

THE SEARCH FOR TREASURE:
THE SIXTH ADVENTURE IN THE KINGDOM OF FANTASY

THE ENCHANTED CHARMS:
THE SEVENTH ADVENTURE IN THE KINGDOM OF FANTASY

THE PHOENIX OF DESTINY:
AN EPIC KINGDOM OF FANTASY ADVENTURE

THE HOUR OF MAGIC:
THE EIGHTH ADVENTURE IN THE KINGDOM OF FANTASY

THE WIZARD'S WAND:
THE NINTH ADVENTURE IN THE KINGDOM OF FANTASY

THE SHIP OF SECRETS:
THE TENTH ADVENTURE IN THE KINGDOM OF FANTASY

THE DRAGON OF FORTUNE:
AN EPIC KINGDOM OF FANTASY ADVENTURE

THE GUARDIAN OF THE REALM:
THE ELEVENTH ADVENTURE IN THE KINGDOM OF FANTASY

THE ISLAND OF DRAGONS:
THE TWELFTH ADVENTURE IN THE KINGDOM OF FANTASY

Visit Geronimo in every universe!

Spacemice

Geronimo Stiltonix and his crew are out of this world!

Cavemice

Geronimo Stiltonoot, an ancient ancestor, is friends with the dinosaurs in the Stone Age!

Micekings

Geronimo Stiltonord lives amongst the dragons in the ancient far north!

ABOUT THE AUTHOR

 Born in New Mouse City, Mouse Island, **GERONIMO STILTON** is Rattus Emeritus of Mousomorphic Literature and of Neo-Ratonic Comparative Philosophy. For the past twenty years, he has been running *The Rodent's Gazette*, New Mouse City's most widely read daily newspaper.

Stilton was awarded the Ratitzer Prize for his scoops on *The Curse of the Cheese Pyramid* and *The Search for Sunken Treasure*. He has also received the Andersen 2000 Prize for Personality of the Year. One of his bestsellers won the 2002 eBook Award for world's best ratling's electronic book. His works have been published all over the globe.

In his spare time, Mr. Stilton collects antique cheese rinds and plays golf. But what he most enjoys is telling stories to his nephew Benjamin.

1. Main entrance
2. Printing presses (where the books and newspaper are printed)
3. Accounts department
4. Editorial room (where the editors, illustrators, and designers work)
5. Geronimo Stilton's office
6. Helicopter landing pad

THE RODENT'S GAZETTE

Map of New Mouse City

1. Industrial Zone
2. Cheese Factories
3. Angorat International Airport
4. WRAT Radio and Television Station
5. Cheese Market
6. Fish Market
7. Town Hall
8. Snotnose Castle
9. The Seven Hills of Mouse Island
10. Mouse Central Station
11. Trade Center
12. Movie Theater
13. Gym
14. Catnegie Hall
15. Singing Stone Plaza
16. The Gouda Theater
17. Grand Hotel
18. Mouse General Hospital
19. Botanical Gardens
20. Cheap Junk for Less (Trap's store)
21. Aunt Sweetfur and Benjamin's House
22. Museum of Modern Art
23. University and Library
24. *The Daily Rat*
25. *The Rodent's Gazette*
26. Trap's House
27. Fashion District
28. The Mouse House Restaurant
29. Environmental Protection Center
30. Harbor Office
31. Mousidon Square Garden
32. Golf Course
33. Swimming Pool
34. Tennis Courts
35. Curlyfur Island Amousement Park
36. Geronimo's House
37. Historic District
38. Public Library
39. Shipyard
40. Thea's House
41. New Mouse Harbor
42. Luna Lighthouse
43. The Statue of Liberty
44. Hercule Poirat's Office
45. Petunia Pretty Paws's House
46. Grandfather William's House

Map of Mouse Island

1. Big Ice Lake
2. Frozen Fur Peak
3. Slipperyslopes Glacier
4. Coldcreeps Peak
5. Ratzikistan
6. Transratania
7. Mount Vamp
8. Roastedrat Volcano
9. Brimstone Lake
10. Poopedcat Pass
11. Stinko Peak
12. Dark Forest
13. Vain Vampires Valley
14. Goose Bumps Gorge
15. The Shadow Line Pass
16. Penny Pincher Castle
17. Nature Reserve Park
18. Las Ratayas Marinas
19. Fossil Forest
20. Lake Lake

21. Lake Lakelake
22. Lake Lakelakelake
23. Cheddar Crag
24. Cannycat Castle
25. Valley of the Giant Sequoia
26. Cheddar Springs
27. Sulfurous Swamp
28. Old Reliable Geyser
29. Vole Vale
30. Ravingrat Ravine
31. Gnat Marshes
32. Munster Highlands
33. Mousehara Desert
34. Oasis of the Sweaty Camel
35. Cabbagehead Hill
36. Rattytrap Jungle
37. Rio Mosquito

Dear mouse friends,
Thanks for reading, and farewell
till the next book.
It'll be another whisker-licking-good
adventure, and that's a promise!

Geronimo Stilton